7-3-02

At the Beach

Anne & Harlow Rockwell

Aladdin Paperbacks

Aladdin Paperbacks
An imprint of Simon & Schuster
Children's Publishing Division
1230 Avenue of the Americas
New York, NY 10020

First Aladdin Paperbacks edition, 1991
4   5   6   7   8   9   10

Printed in Hong Kong

Library of Congress Cataloging-in-Publication Data
Rockwell, Anne F.
At the beach/Anne & Harlow Rockwell.—1st Aladdin Books ed.
p.   cm.
Summary: A child experiences an enjoyable day at the beach
ISBN 0-689-71494-7
[1. Beaches—Fiction.]   I. Rockwell, Harlow.   II. Title.
PZ7.R5943Atm   1991
[E]—dc20   90-45620   CIP   AC

I wear my bathing suit
and I bring my shovel and pail
when I go to the beach.

We bring our towels
and beach umbrella
and tote bag with us.

In the tote bag
there are two cups
and a thermos of lemonade.

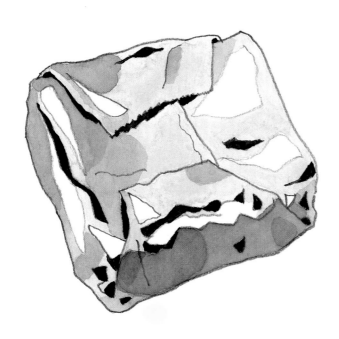
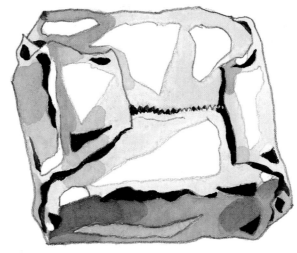

We have two sandwiches
wrapped in aluminum foil
and two peaches for lunch.

There is a tube of sunscreen
to rub on our skin
so we don't get sunburned.
I like the way
the sunscreen smells.

Little sandpipers run
down the beach
and I follow them.

My feet make footprints
in the wet sand.
The sandpipers make footprints, too.

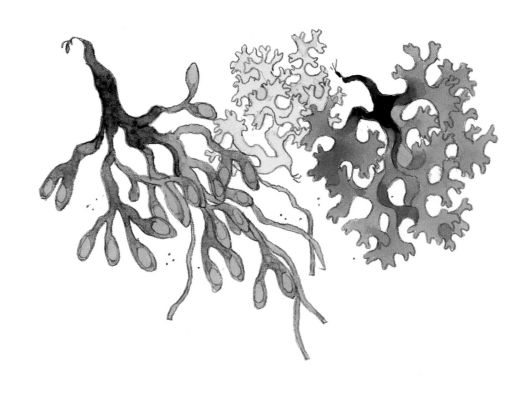

I find some seaweed

and seashells on the beach.

I build a castle with my shovel and pail.
The boy next to me digs a channel
where his boat can float.

Everyone is building something
in the sand at the beach.

I wade in the water.
A little crab tweaks my toe,
and little silver fishes
swim past me.

I like to walk
past the lifeguard's station
to the big, brown rocks.

That is where the barnacles
and snails and mussels live.

When my mother and I go swimming,
the waves crash on us
and get us all wet.
A big sea gull swims close to us.

Then I lie on my towel
and dry myself in the hot sun
until it is time

for lunch.